Published by
PEACHTREE PUBLISHERS, LTD.
1700 Chattahoochee Avenue
Atlanta, Georgia 30318-2112

www.peachtree-online.com

Text © 2000 by Malachy Doyle
Illustrations © 2000 by Paul Hess

First published in Great Britain in 2000 by Andersen Press Ltd.,
20 Vauxhall Bridge Road, London SW1V 2SA.
Published in Australia by Random House Australia Pty.,
20 Alfred Street, Milsons Point, Sydney, NSW 2061.

Printed and bound in Italy by Grafiche AZ, Verona.

10 9 8 7 6 5 4 3 2 1
First Edition

ISBN 1-56145-241-6

Cataloging-in-Publication Data is available from the Library of Congress

HUNGRY! HUNGRY! HUNGRY!

words by Malachy Doyle
with pictures by Paul Hess

PEACHTREE

ATLANTA

Creeping here and crawling there…

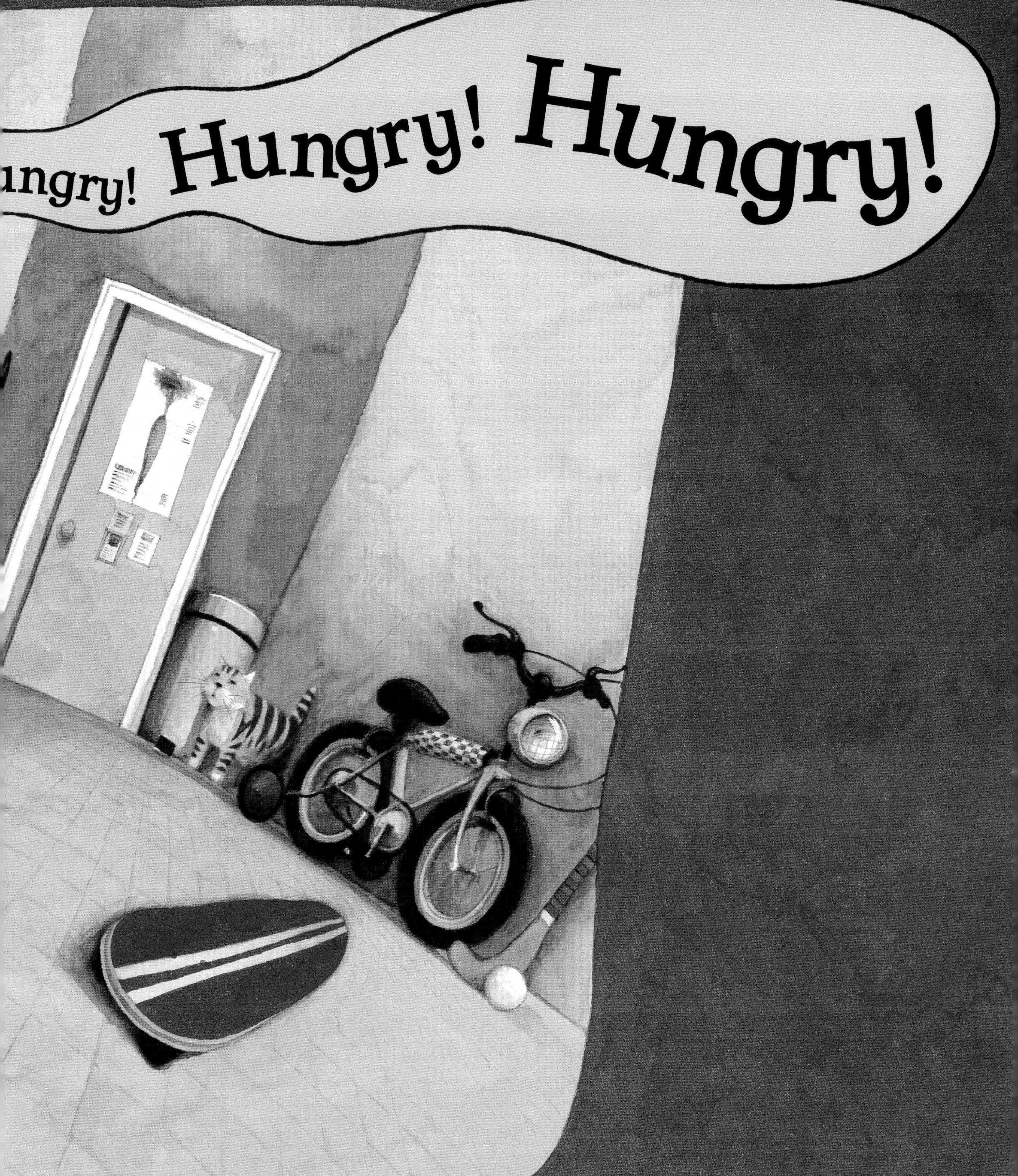
ungry! Hungry! Hungry!

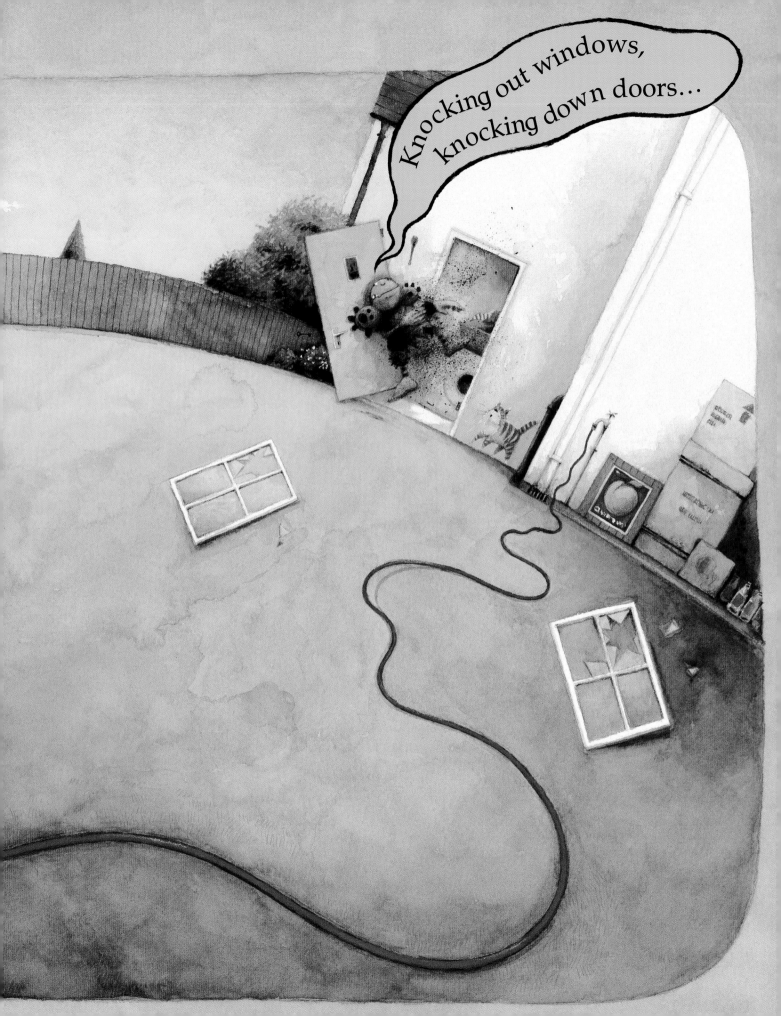

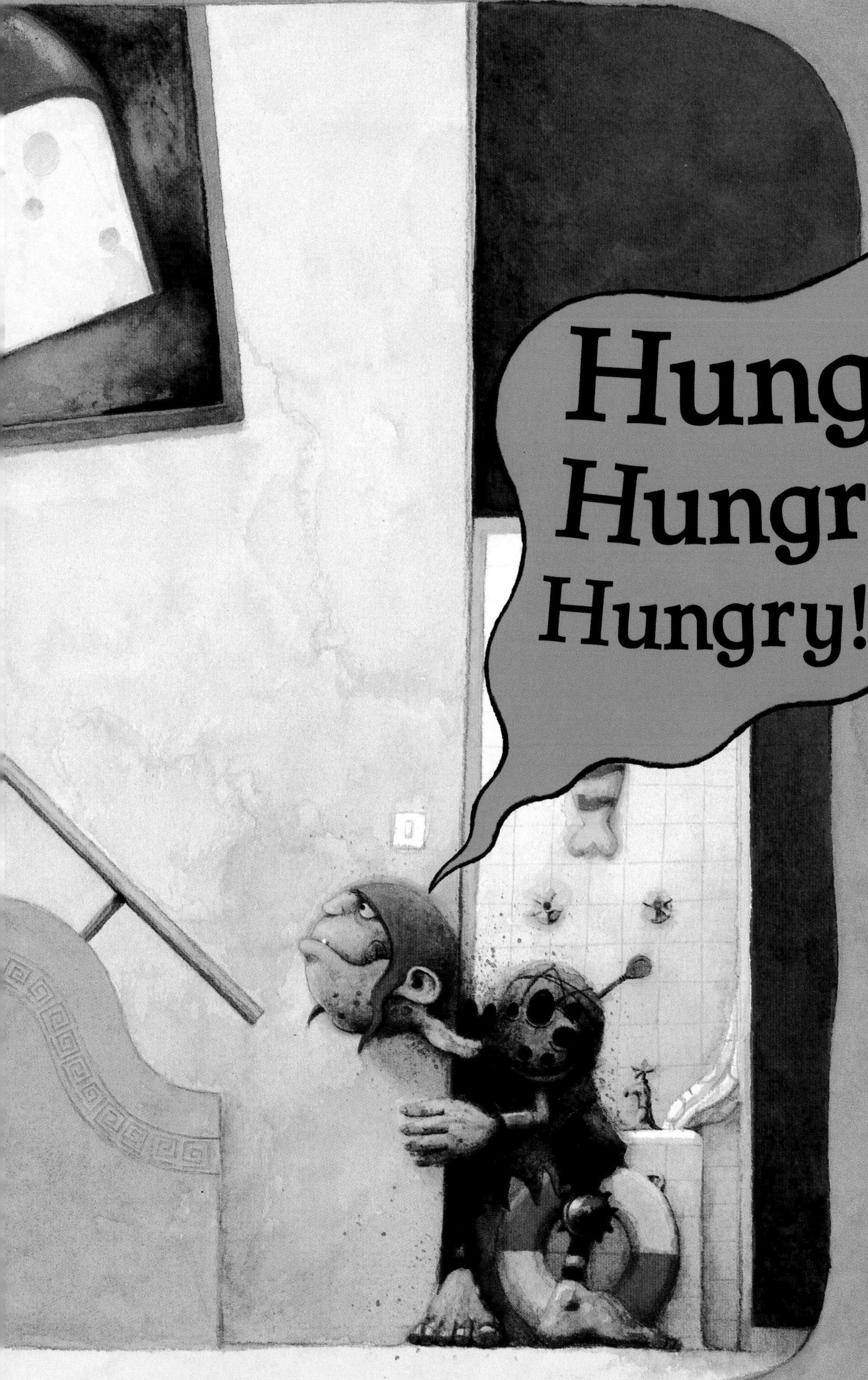
Hungry!
Hungry!
Hungry!